CONTENTS

Tom Tit Tot

A Rumpelstiltskin story,
retold by Joseph Jacobs in *English Fairy Tales*

ONCE UPON A TIME there was a woman who baked five pies. When they came out of the oven, they were that overbaked the crusts were too hard to eat. So she says to her daughter: "Darter, put you them there pies on the shelf, and leave 'em there a little, and they'll come again." She meant, you know, the crust would get soft.

But the girl, she says to herself: "Well, if they'll come again, I'll eat 'em now." And she set to work and ate 'em all, first and last.

Well, come suppertime the woman said: "Go you,

Scary Fairy Tales

The Goblin Pony

and other stories

Compiled by Vic Parker

First published in 2012 by Miles Kelly Publishing Ltd
Harding's Barn, Bardfield End Green, Thaxted, Essex, CM6 3PX, UK

2 4 6 8 10 9 7 5 3 1

Publishing Director Belinda Gallagher
Creative Director Jo Cowan
Editor Sarah Parkin
Designer Jo Cowan
Editorial Assistants Lauren White, Amy Johnson
Production Manager Elizabeth Collins
Reprographics Stephan Davis, Jennifer Hunt, Thom Allaway

ISBN 978-1-84810-595-9

Printed in China

British Library Cataloguing-in-Publication Data
A catalogue record for this book is available from the British Library

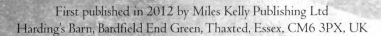

ACKNOWLEDGEMENTS

The publishers would like to thank the following artists who have contributed to this book:

Cover: Iva Sasheva at The Bright Agency
Advocate Art: Luke Finlayson
The Bright Agency: Si Clark, Peter Cottrill, Gerald Kelley, Iva Sasheva

All other artwork from the Miles Kelly Artwork Bank

The publishers would like to thank the following source for the use of their photographs:
Shutterstock.com (cover) donatas1205, Eky Studio; (page decorations) alarik, dmiskv,
Ensuper, Eugene Ivanov, Hal_P

Every effort has been made to acknowledge the source and copyright holder of each picture.
Miles Kelly Publishing apologises for any unintentional errors or omissions.

Made with paper from a sustainable forest

www.mileskelly.net   info@mileskelly.net

www.factsforprojects.com

and get one o' them there pies. I dare say they've come again now."

The girl went and she looked, and there was nothing but the dishes. So back she came, and says she: "Noo, they ain't come again."

"Not one of 'em?" says the mother.

"Not one of 'em," says she.

"Well, come again, or not come again," said the woman, "I'll have one for supper."

"But you can't, if they ain't come," said the girl.

"But I can," says she. "Go you, and bring the best of 'em."

"Best or worst," says the girl, "I've ate 'em all, and you can't have one till that's come again."

Well, the woman she was done, and she took her spinning to the door, and as she span she sang:

"My darter ha' ate five, five pies today.

My darter ha' ate five, five pies today."

The king was coming down the street, and he heard her sing, but what she sang he couldn't hear, so he stopped and said: "What was that you were

singing, my good woman?"

The woman was ashamed to let him hear what her daughter had been doing, so she sang, instead of that:

"My darter ha' spun five, five skeins today.

My darter ha' spun five, five skeins today."

"Stars o' mine!" said the king, "I never heard tell of anyone that could do that."

Then he said: "Look you here, I want a wife, and I'll marry your daughter. But look you here," says he, "eleven months out of the year she shall have all she likes to eat, and all the gowns she likes to get, and all the company she likes to keep; but the last month of the year she'll have to spin five skeins every day, and if she don't, I shall kill her."

"All right," says the woman; for she thought what a grand marriage that was. And as for the five skeins, when the time came, there'd be plenty of ways of getting out of it, and likeliest, he'd have forgotten all about it.

So they were married. And for eleven months the girl had all she liked to eat, and all the gowns she

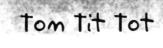

liked to get, and all the company she liked to keep.

But when the time was getting over, she began to think about the skeins and to wonder if he had 'em in mind. But not one word did he say about 'em, and she thought he'd wholly forgotten 'em.

However, the last day of the last month he takes her to a room she'd never set eyes on before. There was nothing in it but a spinning wheel and a stool. And says he: "Now, my dear, here you'll be shut in tomorrow with some victuals and some flax, and if you haven't spun five skeins by the night, your head'll go off." And away he went about his business.

Well, she was that frightened, she'd always been such a careless girl, that she didn't so much as know how to spin, and what was she to do tomorrow with no one to come to help her? She sat down on a stool in the kitchen, and lord, how she did cry!

However, all of a sudden she heard a sort of knocking low down on the door. She upped and opened it, and what should she see but a small little black thing with a long tail, that looked up at her right

curious, and that said: "What are you a-crying for?"

"What's that to you?" says she.

"Never you mind," that said, "but tell me what you're a-crying for."

"That won't do me no good if I do," says she.

"You don't know that," that said, and twirled that's tail round.

"Well," says she, "that won't do no harm, if that don't do no good," and she upped and told about the pies, and the skeins, and everything.

"This is what I'll do," says the little black thing, "I'll come to your window every morning and take the flax and bring it spun at night."

"What's your pay?" says she.

That looked out the corner of that's eyes, and that said: "I'll give you three chances every night to guess my name, and if you haven't guessed it before the month's up, you shall be mine."

Well, she thought she'd be sure to guess that's name before the month was up. "All right," says she, "I agree with you."

"All right," that says, and lord, how that twirled that's tail!

Well, the next day, her husband took her into the room, and there was the flax and the day's food. "Now there's the flax," says he, and if that ain't spun up this night, off goes your head." And then he went out and locked the door.

He'd hardly gone, when there was a knocking against the window. She upped and she opened it, and

there sure enough was the little old thing sitting on the ledge.

"Where's the flax?" says he.

"Here it be," says she, and she gave it to him.

Well, come the evening a knocking came again to the window. She upped and she opened it, and there was the little old thing with five skeins of flax on his arm. "Here it be," says he, and he gave it to her. "Now, what's my name?" says he.

"What, is that Bill?" says she.

"Noo, that ain't," says he, and he twirled his tail.

"Is that Ned?" says she.

"Noo, that ain't," says he, and he twirled his tail.

"Well, is that Mark?" says she.

"Noo, that ain't," says he, and he twirled his tail harder, and away he flew.

Well, when her husband came in, there were the five skeins ready for him. "I see I shan't have to kill you tonight, my dear," says he; "you'll have your food and your flax in the morning," and away he goes.

Well every day the flax and the food were brought,

and every day that there little black imp used to come mornings and evenings. And all the day the girl sat trying to think of names to say to it what it came at night. But she never hit on the right one. And as it got towards the end of the month, the imp began to look so maliceful, and that twirled that's tail faster and faster each time she gave a guess.

At last it came to the last day but one. The imp came at night along with the five skeins, and that said:

"What, ain't you got my name yet?"

"Is that Nicodemus?" says she.

"Noo, 'tain't," that says.

"Is that Sammle?" says she.

"Noo, 'tain't," that says.

"A-well, is that Methusalem?" says she.

"Noo, 'tain't that neither," that says.

Then that looks at her with that's eyes like a coal o' fire, and that says: "Woman, there's only tomorrow night, and then you'll be mine!" And away it flew.

Well, she felt horrid. However, she heard the king coming along the passage.

In he came, and when he sees the five skeins, he says: "Well, my dear, I don't see but what you'll have your skeins ready tomorrow night as well, and as I reckon I shan't have to kill you, I'll have supper in here tonight." So they brought supper, and another stool for him, and down the two sat.

Well, he hadn't eaten but a mouthful or so, when he stops and begins to laugh.

"What is it?" says she.

"A-why," says he, "I was out a-hunting today, and I got away to a place in the wood I'd never seen before. And there was an old chalk pit. And I heard a sort of humming. So I got off my horse, and I went right quiet to the pit, and I looked down. Well, what should there be but the funniest little black thing you ever set eyes on. And what was that doing but that had a little spinning wheel, and that was spinning wonderful fast, and twirling that's tail. And as that span that sang:

'Nimmy nimmy not
My name's Tom Tit Tot'."

Well, when the girl heard this, she felt as if she could have jumped out her skin for joy, but she didn't say a word.

Next day that there little thing looked so maliceful when he came for the flax. And when night came, she heard that knocking against the window panes. She opened the window, and that come right in on the ledge. That was grinning from ear to ear, and ooh, that's tail was twirling round so fast!

"What's my name?" that says.

"Is that Solomon?" she says.

"Noo, 'tain't," that says, and that come further into the room.

"Well, is that Zebedee?" says she yet again.

"Noo, 'tain't," says the imp. And then that laughed and twirled that's tail till you couldn't hardly see it.

"Take time, woman," that says; "next guess, and you're mine." And that stretched out that's black hands at her.

Well, she backed a step or two, and she looked at it, and then she laughed out, and says she, pointing her finger at it:

"Nimmy nimmy not
 Your name's Tom Tit Tot."

Well, when that heard her, that gave an awful shriek and away that flew into the dark, and she never saw it any more.

Beauty and the Beast

From *Europa's Fairy Tales*, Joseph Jacobs

THERE WAS ONCE a merchant who had three daughters. Now it happened that he had to travel on a long journey to buy some goods, and when he was just starting he said to them, "What shall I bring you back, my dears?"

The eldest daughter asked to have a necklace; and the second daughter wished to have a gold chain; but the youngest daughter said, "Bring back yourself, Papa, and that is what I want the most."

"Nonsense, child," said her father, "you must say something that I may bring back for you."

"So," she said, "then bring me back a rose, Father."
The merchant went on his journey and bought a
pearl necklace for his eldest daughter, and a gold
chain for his second daughter; but he knew it was no
use getting a rose for the youngest while he was so far
away because it would fade and die before he got
home. So he made up his mind he would get a rose
for her the day he got near his house, so it stayed
perfect for his beloved daughter.

He forgot all about finding a rose till he was
almost home; then he suddenly remembered what he
had promised his youngest daughter, and looked
about to see if he could find a beautiful bloom. He
saw a great garden, and getting off his horse he
wandered about in it till he found a lovely rose bush;
and he plucked the most beautiful rose he could see
on it. At that moment he heard a sudden crash like
thunder, and looking around he saw a huge monster,
with two tusks sticking out from its mouth, and fiery
eyes surrounded by bristles, and horns coming out of
its head and spreading over its back.

"Mortal," said the Beast, "who told you that you might pluck my roses?"

"Please, sir," said the merchant in fear and terror for his life, "I promised my daughter to bring her home a rose. I saw your beautiful garden and thought you would not miss a single rose, or else I would have asked your permission."

"Thieving is thieving," said the Beast, "whether it be a rose or a diamond; you must pay with your life."

The merchant fell on his knees and begged for his life for the sake of his three daughters who had none but him to work and support them.

"Well, mortal," said the Beast, "I grant your life on one condition: seven days from now you must bring this youngest daughter of yours, for whose sake you have broken into my garden and committed this crime, and leave her here in your place. Otherwise, swear that you will return and that you yourself will become my servant."

So the merchant made his promise and, taking his rose, mounted his horse. As he rode home, his heart was as heavy as lead, his mind full of woe.

As soon as he got into his house his daughters came rushing round him. The merchant tried hard not to show his anxiety and sorrow, and soon he gave the necklace to his eldest daughter, and the chain to his second daughter. But when he gave the rose to his youngest, a deep sigh escaped his lips.

"Oh, thank you, Father," they all cried.

But the youngest said, "Why did you sigh so deeply when you gave me my rose?"

"Later on I will tell you," said the merchant.

So for several days the family got on with everyday life, though the merchant wandered about gloomy and sad. Nothing his daughters could do would cheer him up till at last he took his youngest daughter aside and said to her, "Bella, do you love your father?"

"Of course I do, Father," the maiden replied.

"Well, I have to ask that you do something because you love me," explained the merchant. And then he told her of all that had occurred with the Beast when he got the rose for her.

Bella was very upset, and then she said, "Oh, it was all on account of me that you fell into the power of this Beast; so I will go with you to him; perhaps he will do me no harm; but even if he does, better harm to me than evil to my dear father."

So next day the merchant took Bella on his horse, and they plodded off to the dwelling of the Beast. They allowed the horse to go as slowly as he liked, but the time finally came when they at last arrived. The merchant and his daughter alighted from the horse to find that the doors of the house swung open on their own! So they nervously went up the broad, stone steps and went through the great entrance hall, and went into the grand dining-room, and there they saw a table spread with all manner of beautiful glasses and plates and dishes and cutlery, with plenty to eat upon it. They waited and they waited, thinking that the owner of the house would appear, till at last the merchant said, "Let's sit down and see what will happen then." And when they sat down invisible hands passed them things to eat and to drink, and they ate and drank to their heart's content. When they arose from the table it arose too and disappeared through the door.

Suddenly there appeared before them the Beast, who said to the merchant, "Is this your youngest daughter?" When he was told that it was, he said, "Is she willing to stop here with me?" He looked at Bella who said, in a trembling voice:

"Yes, sir."

"No harm shall befall thee," replied the Beast, and Bella thought that she saw a kind light in his eyes.

With that, he led the merchant down to his horse and told him he might come on the same day the following week to visit his daughter. Then the Beast returned to Bella and said to her, "This house, with everything in it, is yours. If you want anything at all,

just clap your hands and ask for it, and it will be brought to you." And with that he made a sort of bow and went away.

So Bella lived on in the Beast's home of splendour and finery, and was waited on by invisible servants, and had whatever she liked to eat and to drink. The next day, when the Beast came to her, though he looked so terrible, she had been so well treated that she had lost a great deal of her fear of him. So they spoke together about the beautiful garden, and about the house, and about her father's business, and about all manner of things, so that Bella lost altogether her dread of the Beast.

Before Bella knew it, a week had flown by, and her father came to see her. He found her quite happy, and he felt much less worry of her fate at the hands of the Beast. So it went on for many days, Bella talking to the Beast every day, till she got to like him.

One day the Beast did not come at his usual time, and Bella missed him awfully. She searched all over the house, but could find no sign of him at all. So she wandered about the garden trying to find him, calling out his name, but received no reply. Bella's heart began to race with anxiety. Then at last she came to the rose bush from which her father had plucked the rose, and there, under it, was the Beast lying huddled up, without any life or motion. She threw herself down by his side, and began to sob, saying, "Oh, Beast, why did you die? I was getting to

love you so much."

No sooner had she uttered these words than the hide of the Beast split in two and out came the most handsome young prince! He told her that he had been enchanted by a magician and that he could not recover his natural form unless a maiden should, of her own accord, declare that she loved him.

Thereupon the prince sent for the merchant and his daughters, and he was married to Bella, and they all lived happy ever after.

The Goblin Pony

From Andrew Lang's *Grey Fairy Book*

THERE WAS ONCE an old woman named Peggy, whose daughter and husband had died, leaving her to look after her three grandchildren alone. The eldest was a boy who was of the age to want to be out and about by himself. The next grandchild was a daughter, who was kind and hard-working. The youngest grandchild was a boy called Richard, of whom Peggy was especially fond.

One particularly cold, dark night, Peggy felt a chill of fear spread through her old bones, and she gave her grandchildren a solemn warning. "Don't stir from

the fireplace tonight," she said, "for the wind is blowing so violently that the house shakes; besides, this is Halloween, when the witches are abroad and the goblins, who are their servants, are wandering about in all sorts of disguises."

"Why should I stay here?" said the eldest of the young people. "No, I must go and see what the daughter of old Jacob, the rope-maker, is doing."

"I must go and catch lobsters and crabs," said the granddaughter. "If I don't, I will have nothing to sell at market tomorrow."

So they all determined to go on their business or pleasure, and scorned the wise advice of old Peggy. Only the youngest child hesitated a minute, when she said to him, "You stay here, my little Richard, and I will tell you beautiful stories." But he wanted to pick a bunch of wild thyme and some blackberries by moonlight, and ran out after the others.

When they got outside they said, "The old woman talks of wind and storm, but never was the weather finer or the sky more clear!"

Then all of a sudden they noticed a little black pony close beside them.

"Oh, ho!" they said. "That must be old Farmer Valentine's new pony; perhaps it has escaped from its stable and is going down to drink at the pond."

"Pretty pony," said the eldest, "you mustn't run too far; I'll take you to the pond."

With these words he jumped on the pony's back. He was followed by his sister, who reached down a hand and helped little Richard swing himself astride.

Off they set to the pond, trotting along in the moonlight. On the way they met several of their companions, and they invited them all to mount the pony, which they did, and the little creature jogged merrily on.

The quicker it trotted the more the young

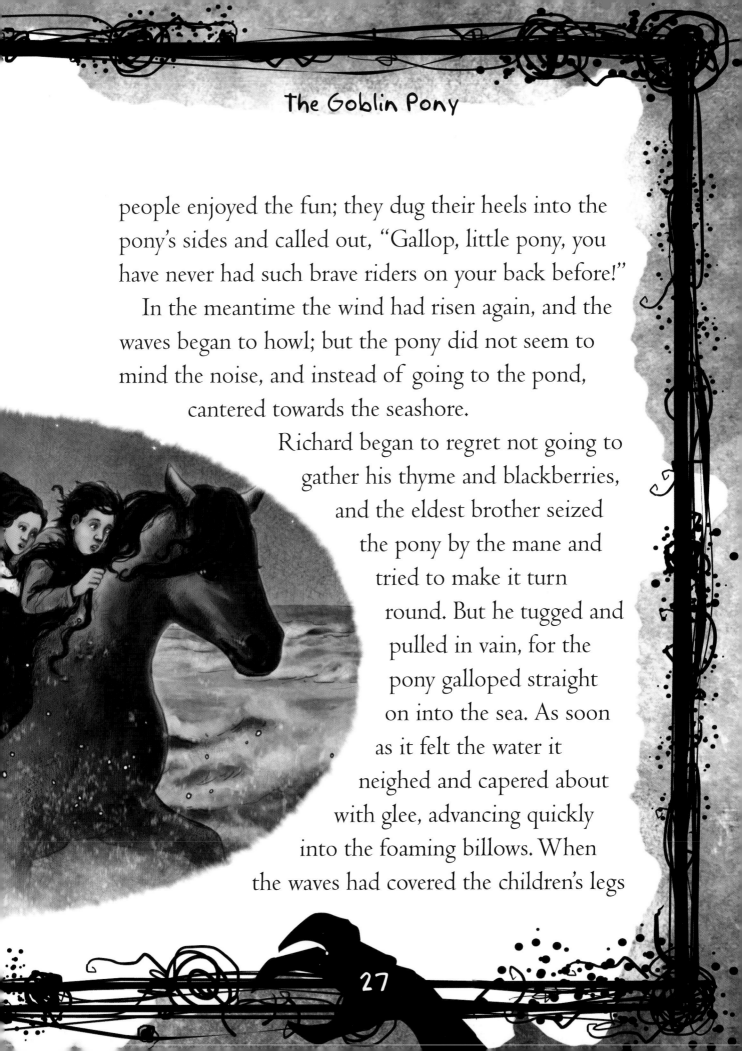

people enjoyed the fun; they dug their heels into the pony's sides and called out, "Gallop, little pony, you have never had such brave riders on your back before!"

In the meantime the wind had risen again, and the waves began to howl; but the pony did not seem to mind the noise, and instead of going to the pond, cantered towards the seashore.

Richard began to regret not going to gather his thyme and blackberries, and the eldest brother seized the pony by the mane and tried to make it turn round. But he tugged and pulled in vain, for the pony galloped straight on into the sea. As soon as it felt the water it neighed and capered about with glee, advancing quickly into the foaming billows. When the waves had covered the children's legs they repented their careless behaviour, and cried out: "The cursed pony is bewitched. If we had only listened to old Peggy's advice we should not have been lost."

The further the pony advanced, the higher rose the sea; at last the waves covered the children's heads and they were all drowned.

Towards morning old Peggy went out, for she was anxious about the fate of her grandchildren. She sought them high and low, but could not find them anywhere. She asked all the neighbours if they had seen the children, but no one knew anything about them. Indeed, several of them were searching for their own missing girls and boys, who had vanished without trace.

As Peggy was going home, bowed with grief, she saw a little black pony coming towards her. When it got near her it neighed loudly, and galloped past her so quickly that in a moment it was out of her sight.

The Jelly Fish and the Monkey

From *Japanese Fairy Tales* by Yei Theodora Ozaki

LONG AGO in old Japan, in the days when the jelly fish was a hard creature with a shell and bones, the oceans were governed by Rin Jin, the Dragon King of the Sea. He was the ruler of all sea creatures, and lived in a palace at the bottom of the ocean. But the Dragon King was not happy, for he reigned on his own and was lonely. Finally he decided to find a wife and called several fish ambassadors to search the oceans for a suitable bride.

At length they brought to the palace a lovely young dragon, with scales like the glittering green of the waves and eyes the gleaming white of pearls, whom the king fell in love with at once. The wedding ceremony was celebrated with great splendour and every living thing in the oceans rejoiced.

The Dragon King and his bride were very happy together – for just two months, for then the Dragon Queen suddenly fell very ill. The desperate king ordered the best doctor and nurses to look after her, but instead of getting better, the young queen grew daily worse. The doctor tried to excuse himself by saying that although he knew the right kind of medicine, it was impossible to find it in the sea.

"Tell me what it is!" demanded the Dragon King.

"The liver cut from a live monkey!" answered the doctor. "If we could only get that, Her Majesty would soon recover."

"Well, even though we sea creatures cannot leave the ocean, we MUST get a monkey to cut up somehow," decided the king.

He called his chief steward for advice, who thought for some time, and declared: "I know! The jelly fish is ugly to look at, but he has a hard shell and four bony legs and can walk on land. An island where there are monkeys lies a few hours' swim to the south — let us send the jelly fish there. If he can't catch a monkey, maybe he can trick one into coming here."

The jelly fish was summoned and ordered to entice a monkey to the Dragon King's palace. Although very worried about the task, the poor jelly fish had no choice but to swim off at once. When he reached Monkey Island he saw a big pine-tree and on one of its branches was a monkey.

"How do you do, Mr Monkey?" called the jelly fish, thinking quickly of a plan. "Isn't it a lovely day?"

"A very fine day," answered the monkey. "I have never seen you before. What is your name?"

"My name is Jelly Fish. I have heard so much of your beautiful island that I have come to see it," answered the jelly fish.

"I am very glad to see you," said the monkey.

"By the bye," said the jelly fish, "have you seen the Palace of the Dragon King of the Sea where I live?"

"I have often heard of it, but I have never seen it!" answered the monkey.

"Then you ought most surely to come. The beauty of the palace is beyond all description – it is certainly the most lovely place in the world," said the jelly fish, and he described the beauty of the Sea King's Palace, the wonders of its garden and the oceans all around.

The monkey grew more and more interested, and came down the tree. "I should love to come with you," he sighed, "but how am I to cross the water? I can't swim."

"There is no difficulty about that. I can carry you on my back," said the jelly fish.

So the excited monkey leaped on to the jelly fish's hard shell and the creature plunged into the sea. Thus they went along, skimming through the waves until they were about halfway, when the jelly fish began to feel more and more sorry for the terrible fate which lay ahead for the monkey. With a sigh, he told the monkey everything – how he was to be killed for his liver, to save the Dragon Queen.

The poor monkey was horrified, and very angry at the trick played upon him. But he was clever, so tried to keep calm and think of some way to escape.

A bright thought struck him, and he said quite cheerfully: "What a pity it was, Mr Jelly Fish, that you did not tell me before we left the island! I have several livers and would happily have given you one – but I have left them all hanging on the pine-tree."

The jelly fish was very disappointed, for he

believed the story.

"Never mind," said the monkey, "take me back to where you found me and I will fetch a liver."

The pleased jelly fish turned his course towards Monkey Island once more. But no sooner had he reached the shore than the sly monkey scampered up into the pine-tree and jeered at him. "Of course, I won't GIVE you my liver, but come and get it if you can!" mocked the monkey.

There was nothing for the jelly fish to do but return to the Dragon King and confess his failure.

The Dragon King was beside himself with fury. He ordered a terrible punishment: that all the bones were to be drawn out from the jelly fish's body, that he was to be beaten with sticks until his shell broke off and he was left a flattened pulp, then banished from the palace.

The jelly fish cried out for pardon. But the Dragon King's order had to be obeyed. And that is why, ever since, the descendents of the jelly fish have all been soft and boneless, just as you see them today.

The Strange Visitor

From Joseph Jacobs' *English Fairy Tales*

A WOMAN WAS SITTING at her reel one night;

And still she sat, and still she reeled, and still she wished for company.

In came a pair of broad broad feet, and sat down at the fireside;

And still she sat, and still she reeled, and still she wished for company.

In came a pair of small small legs, and sat down on the broad broad feet;

And still she sat, and still she reeled, and still she

wished for company.

In came a pair of thick thick knees, and sat down on the small small legs;

And still she sat, and still she reeled, and still she wished for company.

In came a pair of thin thin thighs, and sat down on the thick thick knees;

And still she sat, and still she reeled, and still she wished for company.

In came a pair of huge huge hips, and sat down on the thin thin thighs;

And still she sat, and still she reeled, and still she wished for company.

In came a wee wee waist, and sat down on the huge huge hips;

And still she sat, and still she reeled, and still she wished for company.

In came a pair of broad broad shoulders, and sat down on the wee wee waist;

And still she sat, and still she reeled, and still she wished for company.

In came a pair of small small arms, and sat down on the broad broad shoulders;

And still she sat, and still she reeled, and still she wished for company.

In came a pair of huge huge hands, and sat down on the small small arms;

And still she sat, and still she reeled, and still she wished for company.

In came a small small neck, and sat down on the broad broad shoulders;

And still she sat, and still she reeled, and still she wished for company.

In came a huge huge head, and sat down on the small small neck.

"How did you get such broad broad feet?" quoth the woman.

"Much tramping, much tramping." (*gruffly*)

"How did you get such small small legs?"

"Aih-h-h!-late—and wee-e-e—moul." (*whiningly*)

"How did you get such thick thick knees?"

"Much praying, much praying." (*piously*)

"How did you get such thin thin thighs?"

"Aih-h-h!—late—and wee-e-e—moul." (*whiningly*)

"How did you get such huge huge hips?"

"Much sitting, much sitting." (*gruffly*)

"How did you get such a wee wee waist?"

"Aih-h-h!—late—and wee-e-e-moul." (*whiningly*)

"How did you get such broad broad shoulders?"

"With carrying broom, with carrying broom." (*gruffly*)

"How did you get such small small arms?"

"Aih-h-h!—late—and wee-e-e—moul." (*whiningly*)

"How did you get such huge huge hands?"

"Threshing with an iron flail, threshing with an iron flail." (*gruffly*)

"How did you get such a small small neck?"

"Aih-h-h!—late—wee-e-e—moul." (*pitifully*)

"How did you get such a huge huge head?"

"Much knowledge, much knowledge." (*keenly*)

"What do you come for?"

(*At the top of the voice, with a wave of the arm and a stamp of the feet.*) "FOR YOU!"